THE CASE OF THE UNSUITABLE SUITOR

A 1920S HISTORICAL COZY MYSTERY

THE KITTY WORTHINGTON COZY CAPERS
BOOK THREE

MAGDA ALEXANDER

Beaux Aires Publishing

CHAPTER 1

London, Eaton Square
March 1924

FROSTY BEGINNINGS AT THE LADIES OF
DISTINCTION

"*B*rrrr," I said, rushing into the Ladies of Distinction Detective Agency, the business I owned. "It's beyond freezing out there."

Lady Emma, my friend and business partner, was not far behind. "If this cold snap lasts much longer, we'll have icicles hanging off the tips of our noses."

Betsy, our agency receptionist, and my former lady's maid, who'd brought up the rear asked as soon as she stepped inside, "Shall I put the kettle on?"

"Absolutely. Thank you, Betsy," I said.

For sundry reasons, the three of us lived at my family's residence, Worthington House. Most mornings, we traveled to the office together in my roadster. However, given the frigid temperatures, that would not have been a comfortable choice today. So Neville, the Worthington chauffeur and Betsy's beau, had driven us in the family's Rolls Royce.

"I hope this cold snap ends soon," I said after hanging my coat in the foyer wardrobe. "It makes it dash difficult to conduct our investigations."

"Indeed," Lady Emma said, peeling off her gloves. "Well, at least the agency is warm."

Thanks to the gas heating the owner had installed. It had been one of the more important factors in my decision to lease the Eaton Square townhouse. While other addresses I'd inspected had been larger and less expensive, none had all the modern conveniences of this building.

"Good morning, ladies," Lady Aurelia Holmes, the agency's newest lady detective, said from the stairs. A recent hire, we'd offered her the top floor of the townhouse for her personal use as her living quarters, a thoroughly comfortable arrangement as it allowed her privacy and came rent-free. Something she greatly appreciated as she'd found herself penniless after her father's death. In the short time she'd been with us, she'd more than proven herself.

"Good morning," we all answered in unison.

Before we had a chance to say more, a rat-a-tat-tat sounded on the front door. One of the delivery boys from the Tea and Tattle Shoppe with our daily morning delivery of scones, tea cakes, and pastries.

Soon we were gathered in Lady Emma's office, enjoying hot cups of tea and delicious treats while we reviewed our caseload. A daily ritual we all enjoyed.

"Goodness, I said, "Do we really have ten cases between us?"

"Afraid so," Lady Emma said. "A consequence of all the publicity the agency has received from the press. When a pesky problem arises, especially among the nobility, we are the ones they seek. And not only those. Just yesterday we received an enquiry from Sir Frederick Stone."

The solicitor who'd represented my fiancé when Robert had been wrongfully incarcerated. Sir Frederick had been so impressed with my investigative skills, he'd promised to engage us in future enquiries. This was the first of hopefully many. "What does it involve?"

"He wants to know if a certain individual has been involved in a criminal matter."

"Assign that task to Mister Clapham," I said. "Given his connections at Scotland Yard, that should be easily determined." I'd hired him to help me develop my investigative skills, something he was well versed in as a former detective inspector. Since then, he'd also become a dear friend.

"Exactly my thinking," Lady Emma said. "I will talk to him this morning."

"What about you, Lady Aurelia? Anything new to report?"

A wrinkle appeared on Lady Aurelia's brow. "The Millwood matter is proving particularly thorny."

"How so?"

"Lord Millwood refuses to see me."

The heir to an earldom had gotten a young woman in trouble. When told she was in the family way, he'd told her to get rid of it. She'd refused to do so and had given birth to a boy. Her mother, who'd stood by her through the ordeal, wanted him to pay for the child's upkeep and provide a modest allowance to compensate the young woman whose life he'd ruined.

"I wish we could leak it to the papers," I said. "Let the world know what a cad he is."

"Society won't care," Lady Emma responded. "They thrive on scandals. It's bound to hurt our client more than him, and she's suffered enough already."

Suddenly, I remembered something I'd seen. "Maybe not."

"What do you mean?" Lady Emma asked.

"There was a notice in the paper this morning. I read it over my morning coffee." Coming to my feet, I approached Betsy. "Has the Tittle Tattle arrived?" We had subscriptions to all the London newspapers, including the rags that thrived on gossip and scandals.

"Yes, Miss." Going through the pile, she chose one and handed it to me.

After finding what I needed, I placed the newspaper on the desk. "Here, see." The headline of the article read— *Wedding bells for a Peer and a Yank?* "Apparently, he's offered for Miss Penelope Ross, the American railroad tycoon's daughter. If she were to learn he seduced an innocent and got her with child, she might very well call off the engagement."

"Oh, she definitely would," Lady Emma said after perusing the report. "She appears to be a devout Christian."

"Lady Aurelia, write to him again. And this time, include that article. Once he sees it, he'll come around fast enough."

"That's brilliant, Kitty."

"Add ten percent to whatever figure that young woman's mother is requesting. No, make it twenty. Make him pay through the nose."

"I'll do that immediately. If you'll excuse me," Lady Aurelia dashed out.

No sooner had she done so than Mister Clapham arrived.

"Good morning." He rubbed his hands as he doffed his hat and coat. "Could use a cuppa, Betsy."

"Coming right up, Mister Clapham."

Once Betsy handed him a steaming cup of tea, he walked into Lady Emma's office. "Got anything for me?"

"As a matter of fact," Lady Emma said.

Leaving her to explain the new assignment, I stepped out

of her office and into my own as there were some things I needed to do.

Two hours later, Betsy knocked on my door, "Excuse me, Miss. It's Lord Robert on the phone."

The man I loved and my fiancé. "Patch him through, and please close the door, Betsy."

"Yes, Miss."

I held the receiver to my ear and waited to be connected. Some crackling sounds later, I said, "Robert?"

"Hello, darling. How are you?"

"Busy. You won't believe how many matters we're investigating."

"Same."

"Not too busy to miss supper tonight, I hope." Mother was holding a special dinner party to celebrate Father's birthday. Our entire family, sans my brother Richard, who was in Egypt, would be there. She looked upon Robert as part of the family and would be disappointed if he didn't attend.

"I'll be there."

I sensed hesitation in his voice. "Is something wrong?"

"I've been assigned to a special case. Unfortunately, it means I'll be undercover for the near future."

That did not sound good. "What does that mean?"

"After tonight, I may not see you until the matter is resolved."

We'd just reunited after he'd been wrongfully detained for a murder he did not commit. The last thing I wished was to be separated again. "How long will that take?"

"I don't know, Catherine. I wish I did."

Bother!

CHAPTER 2

AN UNEXPECTED INVITATION

That evening was especially poignant. After supper, our family and friends sang "Happy Birthday" to Father while Cook herself delivered a birthday cake that resembled Sir Winston, his beloved basset hound. She'd even baked Sir Winston a smaller one so he wasn't left out of the celebration. While most of the family and friends laughed, Mother frowned. Sir Winston had never been a favorite of hers after he suffered an unfortunate accident on a valuable Aubusson rug.

After the entire supper party retired to the drawing room, I held tightly to Robert's hand. The thought of being separated from him after everything we'd gone through the previous month was too much to bear. We engaged in desultory conversation while avoiding the subject that was uppermost in our minds. It would not have done any good to ask him about his undercover assignment. Its secretive nature prevented him from discussing it in public. But at the end of the evening, when family and guests finally drifted away, I once again expressed my disappointment. "I wish you did not have to take on this assignment. I hate being apart."

He cupped a hand on my cheek. "I don't believe it will be long, darling."

I sighed. "I hope so."

When it was time to say our goodnights, I accompanied him to the front door. We did not engage in a passionate embrace. We'd already enjoyed that in the drawing room. So Robert simply placed a last kiss on my cheek before making his way out. Once he'd gone, I climbed the stairs to my room where it took me hours to fall asleep.

The following morning, spring decided to make an appearance as the cold temperatures gave way to warmer ones. The budding blooms on the trees lifted my spirits, providing me with the hope I would see Robert again soon.

After we arrived at the agency, Lady Emma, as well as Lady Aurelia, left to investigate different matters. Since one of us had to remain in the office in case a prospective client showed up, I spent the morning writing progress reports of my ongoing enquiries. This was something Lady Emma insisted upon. It not only lent support to our billing but provided evidence when matters came before courts of law, such as divorce proceedings. It was one of the main reasons we were able to charge higher rates.

As it turned out, it was fortunate I'd remained at my desk. Two hours into the morning, I received a telephone call from the Foreign Affairs Office. The Under Secretary wanted to discuss something with me. I wasn't asked but was told they were sending a government car for me. I was to tell no one where I was going. The meeting was set for eleven, and it was just about that time now.

No sooner had the call ended than another one came through. Lord Salverton. A recent acquaintance from the

Oxford investigation. I'd divined he worked in Intelligence for our government. I did not wonder why he was calling.

"Salverton. How pleasant to hear from you."

"Thank you. I trust you're in good health," he replied in that deep voice of his.

"I am." I briefly paused. "Now that we've observed the niceties, shall we talk about the reason you telephoned?"

He laughed. "I knew I couldn't get anything past you."

"Thank you."

"You received a call from the Foreign Affairs Office," he said.

I didn't even wonder how he knew. "I did."

"It's bona fide. The Under Secretary of Foreign Affairs wants to meet with you."

"Any idea why?"

"No. And, even if I knew, I could not share it with you. But you'll learn the reason soon enough."

"Very well. Thanks for the reassurance I won't be kidnapped by white slave traders."

He laughed again. "You're welcome." And with that, he ended the call.

Several minutes later, Betsy was knocking on my office door. "A Mister Brown has arrived. He says he's come to fetch you?" Her eyes were as big as saucers.

"Yes, Betsy. Thank you." With seemingly no recourse but to obey the edict, I retrieved my coat, hat, and gloves from the foyer wardrobe and followed Mister Brown out the door. But before stepping out, I said, "If I don't return in two hours, ask Lady Emma to contact Lord Salverton."

I knew better than to ask questions of 'Mister Brown' if that was even his name. So the ride to the Foreign Affairs Office was conducted in silence. Once we arrived at that impressive building, I was escorted through the labyrinth of hallways to a lift which took us to the top floor. After a swift knock on the door, Mister Brown waited only long enough for someone to open the door before leaving.

The young gentleman in front of me introduced himself as Mister White—honestly, these government types had no imagination. After informing me the Under Secretary was delayed, he pointed to a small sofa where I could wait. After what seemed an interminable length of time, but in reality, was only fifteen minutes, I was shown to the inner sanctum where a tall, distinguished-looking gentleman with mahogany hair came to his feet as soon as I stepped into the room.

"Miss Worthington. Thank you for coming on such short notice." Coming around to my side, he held out his hand, "I'm Phillip Rickard, the Under Secretary of Foreign Affairs."

I shook his hand. "Mister Rickard."

"Shall we sit?" He pointed to a seating arrangement comprised of one settee, two facing chairs, and a rectangular table in between.

Once we'd chosen our seats, Mister White entered with a tea service comprised of two carafes, sugar, cream, lemon . . . and three cups and saucers. Someone would be joining us. At this point, I wouldn't be surprised if His Majesty King George V himself walked into the room.

Once Mister White served the refreshments, he quit the room. Rather than broach the subject of my visit, Mister Rickard engaged in desultory conversation—the vagaries of the British weather was always a safe subject. A few minutes later, another knock sounded on the door, and an individual stepped into the room. Imagine my surprise when I recognized "Robert!"

"Hello, Catherine." He kissed my cheek and took the space next to me on the settee.

The Under Secretary waited until Robert helped himself

to coffee before he spoke. "Miss Worthington, you must be curious as to why you're here."

An understatement of the highest magnitude. "Yes, Sir. I am."

"We have a request to make of you."

"We?" I asked.

"The Foreign Affairs office." He paused for a moment, more than likely to gather his thoughts. "Have you heard of the Kingdom of Zenovia?"

"A small country in Europe."

"Strategically located between Germany and Italy. We enjoy very pleasant relations with His Majesty, the King of Zenovia, as well as its government." After a brief pause, he continued. "We'd like to keep it that way."

"But something has come along to challenge the status quo."

The Under Secretary's eyes crinkled at the corners. "Lord Robert mentioned how perceptive you are."

I glanced at my fiancé. "Did he indeed?"

A small smile was Robert's only answer.

"Which is one of the reasons you've been chosen for this mission."

'Mission' sounded downright clandestine, and that perked me up to no end. "Oh?"

"What do you know about Princess Elena of Zenovia?"

"She's in England at the moment. In a private boarding school. Longworth, I believe."

"That's correct. Since she's to be the Queen of Zenovia, her parents felt she needed to enlarge her worldview. They enrolled her at Longworth when she was sixteen years old."

"I read about it in the press while I was at a boarding school myself."

"L'école des Dames de Distinction in Lausanne," Rickard said, correctly naming the institution I'd attended.

When I arched a questioning brow, he said, "Young ladies can be particularly vulnerable to foreign influences. We like to stay informed."

Good heavens! Had they planted a spy at my finishing school?

"Six months ago, the princess moved into a private residence to prepare for her debut season. Something her parents wanted her to experience before she returned to Zenovia. She's expected to marry a duke, chosen for her when she was born."

It was madness to choose a husband at a child's birth, but such was the way of royals.

"Unfortunately, her chaperone, a lady from the Zenovia court, was not as vigilant as she should have been. The princess, an accomplished equestrienne, was allowed to roam the countryside on horseback with only a stable lad for company. Not exactly a proper escort." Rickard's brow furrowed. "During her wanderings, she encountered a gentleman from a neighboring estate, and she fell in love. While of noble lineage, he's quite unacceptable as the husband of the princess. But she's set her heart on him. We positioned several members of the government in the house she's currently occupying. They tell us the princess and the gentleman are planning to elope sometime in the near future."

"That would be a disaster, I gather," I said, taking a sip of coffee.

"Of the highest magnitude. The princess is under our care while on British soil. Her father, the King of Zenovia, might very well sever relations with Great Britain if this elopement takes place."

"So why do you need my help? What could I possibly do?"

"To put it plainly, Miss Worthington," Rickard said with a

11

gleam in his eyes, "we want you to seduce the cad away from the princess."

CHAPTER 3

A DANGEROUS MISSION

*M*y cup rattled on the saucer. Thankfully, I caught it before the liquid landed on the no-doubt priceless Aubusson rug. "I beg your pardon!"

"It's not that at all, Catherine," Robert said before turning to the Under Secretary. "Jester, that was quite inappropriate."

"Jester!" I exclaimed. Robert had told me about the pranks a fellow Oxford student liked to play on others. "Is he who I think he is?"

Robert nodded. "Sir Phillip Rickard, Jester to his mates."

"You were at Oxford with Robert where you liked to play silly pranks."

He offered a lopsided smile. "Guilty as charged, Miss Worthington. I do apologize. But you were so serious I thought a bit of levity was necessary."

I arched a brow. "I did not appreciate the joke."

"My apologies," Rickard said, still wearing an amused grin. Obviously, he wasn't the least bit sorry.

"May I explain?" Robert asked of Jester.

Rickard nodded while pouring more tea into his cup.

"The goal of the mission is to prove what a cad Lord Farringer is. That's the gentleman who attracted the princess's notice. To give you a bit of a background, his estate is deeply in debt. So, he's in desperate need of funds. His reason for marrying the princess is to gain access to the dowry she's due upon her marriage. Over 300,000 pounds."

"Good heavens!" I knew the country of Zenovia was rich in natural resources, but I had no idea of the vast expanse of its wealth.

"Exactly," Robert agreed. "However, she must marry with the approval of the King of Zenovia. Something he's threatening to withhold."

"So why would Farringer want to marry her? Without her father's approval, the marriage is not likely to take place."

"He's counting on the king changing his mind."

"Why would he do that?"

"The princess is the king's only child. By all accounts, he loves her dearly. But the king has his own ace to play."

"What is that?"

"If the king disapproves of the marriage, he can declare her unfit for the throne. And that means she would never be queen, something she very much wants and has been raised to expect. He's counting on his daughter's desire for the crown to overcome her attraction to Lord Farringer."

"Does he know of his daughter's plans to marry?"

Rickard brushed a nonexistent piece of lint from his trousers. "He does and sent an emissary to remind her she needs his approval to marry. So far, she's refused to change her mind. Needless to say, he's not happy about the course of events. He blames us for allowing this to happen and demands we do everything in our power to stop the wedding to Lord Farringer. Once that has occurred, he will send an envoy to fetch the princess home."

The woman in me rebelled. "So she can marry the duke? Shouldn't she be given a choice as to who she marries?"

Rickard leaned forward. "The man the king chose for her consort is a good, noble man, Miss Worthington. Not only would he treat her with kindness, but he approves of an alliance with the United Kingdom. He will make her an excellent husband."

I sensed our government was afraid of more than a rift between the two countries. "But there's more to this."

A gleam of admiration shone in Rickard's eyes. "You're right. If the princess does not inherit the throne, her cousin will become king. A quite despicable fellow who opposes an alliance with the United Kingdom. He prefers Germany."

I frowned. "And that, of course, is something we cannot allow."

"Exactly so."

After a few moments to ponder what he said, I asked, "So how do I fit into this scheme?"

"You will assume the identity of a young widow. After a marriage that only lasted six months, your husband was tragically killed in a riding accident. Your dowry, worth over 100,000 pounds, was left practically untouched. It cannot descend to your husband's heir as your wealthy tycoon of a father specifically tied it to you and not your husband. You wish for children, something you did not manage during your marriage, so you are coming to London to find a new spouse."

"That's all well and good, but I just enjoyed a season. Everyone who is anyone knows me."

"You will be heavily disguised. Your wig will be a mousy shade of blonde. You will have heavy eyebrows. Your personality will also undergo a drastic change. You will be quiet, demure, unassuming, everything you are not. Not even your mother will recognize you."

Somehow I doubted that. "But given my lack of beauty, how would I attract a man like Lord Farringer?"

"He needs money. You are more than willing to hand over your fortune once you marry. We have arranged for Lady Darlington, a close friend of the Foreign Affairs office, to act as your sponsor. She will introduce you to him and let it be known you're looking for a second husband as you want children. You wish to marry someone with a title, so Farringer fits the bill. Although Farringer is deemed attractive and charming, neither is important to you. The only thing that matters is the ability to father a child."

"And how would I know he can do that?"

"He has illegitimate offspring already."

I gritted my teeth. "Does he really?"

"Farringer is a cad of the worst sort. He takes advantage of innocents, including members of his household staff. He's gotten at least two of them with child. Not only didn't he stand up to his responsibilities, but he dismissed them as soon as he discovered they were in the family way."

I hissed out a harsh breath. "I hate that sort of men. So how will this subterfuge be accomplished?"

"We'll set you up in a lavish residence across from Regent's Park. Lady Darlington will introduce you to society as a dear friend, a wealthy widow who lost her husband two years ago. You loved him dearly but there were no children from the union. And you would dearly love a child."

"That will take time, won't it?"

"Lady Darlington is already spreading the word about the new rich widow in town. Members of the nobility can't help but be drawn to a lady with an air of mystery about her, so invitations are already pouring in. Everyone is eager to meet the mysterious Mrs. Woolrich."

I glanced toward my fiancé. "What about Robert? I assume he will be part of this."

Robert squeezed my hand. "I'll be by your side the entire time, darling, an uncle eager to bat away your admirers."

"Why?"

He grinned. "If you die childless, I inherit the lot."

I smiled. "So you're the villain of the piece."

"Indeed." He bared his teeth. "I'm quite looking forward to playing that role."

"Do try not to kill them, Robbie," Rickard said. "It'd be the very devil to clean that up."

"Robbie?" That was a new moniker for him.

Robert shrugged.

"So what do you say, Miss Worthington? Are you game?"

Game. Why was it men always phrased this sort of thing in sporting terms? "I will need a private word with Robert before I decide."

Rickard came to his feet. "By all means." He glanced at his pocket watch. "I have a meeting to attend. Will thirty minutes suffice?"

"That should be plenty of time. Thank you."

"No. Thank you, Miss Worthington." And with that, he bowed and left.

"Was this the assignment you told me about?" I asked Robert.

He nodded.

"So we'll be together the entire time?"

"Yes. We will live in the same house, enjoy all our meals together, and take walks in the garden."

I grinned. "So it would be similar to being married without actually being married."

"Except for the intimate parts, of course."

He would say that, but then I didn't expect any less of him. "You make this sound awfully tempting."

"I mean to do so. This is really important, Catherine. We can't afford for Zenovia to ally with Germany." He paused. "And there's more."

"More?" How complicated could this thing be?

"Farringer is suspected of involvement in shady dealings adverse to British interests. Unfortunately, we haven't been able to discover any proof."

"And you hope that my acquaintance with him would get you that proof?"

"Yes."

"But how will this work? I can't very well lead a double life. My family would have to know."

"I'll talk to your father and mother. No one else needs to be aware of the situation."

"But what possible excuse could I give for my absence to everyone else?"

"You've been asked to perform a delicate mission by the government which necessitates travel away from London. You don't know how long you'll be gone."

"But people will recognize me. I only made my debut last year."

"By the time we're through disguising you, no one will recognize you."

I scoffed. "Some members of society are very observant. They might very well winkle out my identity."

"The makeup artists assigned to this mission are the very best at disguising people. They will make sure that doesn't happen."

"When would this mission start?"

"Tomorrow morning a car will arrive at Worthington House. The driver will take you to Paddington Station. Once you arrive there, an agent will meet you and whisk you to your new Regent's Park residence."

"What about you?"

"I will be there to welcome you. We will have a full complement of staff at our disposal, including a butler, housekeeper, chauffeur, maids, footmen, and even a gardening crew."

"All of whom work for the government?"

"Yes."

"What happens if I say no?"

"You leave and carry on with your life."

"My detective agency is extremely busy. I can't just leave them in the lurch."

"We will do what we can to resolve matters. Lord Millwood, for example, has already received a visit. You'll find he's amenable to your proposal."

Heavens! They knew everything.

"In the future, when a particular issue comes up where your agency can be of use, the government will send business your way. I demanded that for you."

"Thank you." It would be a feather in the agency's cap to handle such tasks. "What happens if I say yes?"

"We'll spend the rest of the day instructing you in your new role. You'll meet those important staff members who will run your household—the butler, the housekeeper, cook, and chauffeur. The last one is very important. You will go nowhere without him."

As tempting as the offer was, I hesitated to accept it. "I don't know what to do, Robert. I want to help but this seems like too high a mountain to climb."

"If you're not completely convinced, turn down the offer. No one will blame you, least of all me."

"What happens if I say no?"

"They have another lady in mind."

"Who?"

"Lady Felicia Endecott."

"During our debut season, she was always up for a lark, so she'll more than likely accept the assignment."

"She doesn't have your intelligence, your daring, or your smile. I think she'll bottle it."

"Yes, she very likely would. But why can't they simply assign one of their agents to this operation?"

"Because it has to be a lady who knows the rules of society, even if she sometimes breaks those rules." He finished with a grin.

I flashed him a smile of my own. "I wouldn't be arrested if I do a little breaking and entering?"

"If you do, I know someone who can get you out."

"Why, Inspector" — I curled my arms around him — "You'd do that for me?"

"And King and Country, my love." He spent the next few minutes showing me just how much he cared.

"The agency will suffer," I said once I came up for air.

"The government will make sure it doesn't."

"Mother will be upset."

"I believe she'll accept it as long as you're not hurt."

"And my reputation doesn't suffer."

"If there's any chance of either happening, I will pull you out."

"How?"

"Clara Woolrich would become ill and retire to the country."

"But what about the mission?"

"Bother the mission. You're more important to me than the entire country of Zenovia."

"We *would* get to be together all the time."

"You in your room and me on the other side of the house with my door firmly locked."

I glanced up at him through my lashes. "Even when I use my womanly wiles?"

"Even so. This is serious business, Catherine. We can't muff it up."

"Oh, very well."

"So, what do you want to do?"

I grinned. "Accept, of course."

He smiled back. "Farringer won't know what hit him."

CHAPTER 4

FIRST STEPS INTO THE HIGH SOCIETY TRAP

*R*obert and I paused for a moment at the top of the grand marble staircase of Lady Langham's mansion. Our first public outing was her ball.

"Mrs. Clara Woolrich and Mister Gerald Vale," the stentorian tones of the butler declared loudly to everyone gathered below.

I took a deep breath and, with my hand firmly curled around Robert's arm, descended the steps. The air was thick with the scent of expensive perfume, laughter, and the hum of chatter, a perfect setting for the intrigue I'd been tasked to unravel.

Tonight, I wasn't Kitty Worthington, the astute sleuth of the Ladies of Distinction Detective Agency. Tonight, I was Mrs. Clara Woolrich, a widow new to the glittering world of high society. A world filled with opulence and power, but also deception and ulterior motives.

I swept a gaze across the ballroom, taking in the glittering chandeliers, the aristocratic crowd, and the sight of ladies adorned in shimmering gowns of the latest Parisian fashion. It was all part of the spectacle. But I knew better than to be mesmerized by the glamour. The real game was played beneath the surface, in whispered conversations and hidden glances.

"Which one is Lord Farringer?" I asked Robert.

"The dark-haired dandy standing on the right surrounded by a bevy of women."

He wasn't difficult to find as he was indeed in the center of several adoring ladies, all eager to gain his attention. His presence was magnetic, with a face that could have been sculpted by an artist, all sharp angles and aristocratic features. His dark hair, streaked with silver at the temples, only added to his air of distinction. The circle of admirers who surrounded him laughed at something he said, but it was clear he held little regard for them. He wore an expression of mild amusement, as if everything around him was a game.

Once we reached the bottom, Lady Darlington, who I'd met the day before, approached me. "Mrs. Woolrich, how lovely to see you."

I curtsied and she did as well. "Thank you, Lady Darlington." I'd adopted a softer voice than my usual, making me sound shyer, less sure of myself.

"We seem to have struck a bit of luck," Lady Darlington said in a low tone.

"How so?" I asked.

"The princess was not able to attend. Apparently, she's a bit under the weather. So we won't have to worry about prying her away from Farringer."

Well, that certainly made my job easier.

Turning to Robert, she said, "Felix Larkspur, a particular associate of Farringer is here. You can't miss him. Shock of red hair, dressed abominably. You'll want to search him out."

"Will do." Robert bowed his head and left me in Lady Darlington's hands.

Linking arms with me, Lady Darlington led me to Lord Farringer's side. Thankfully, his bevy of admirers had faded away, leaving him for the moment standing alone.

As we approached, Farringer's gaze fell upon me. For a brief moment, something flickered in his eyes—curiosity, perhaps? Interest? My heart quickened, though not out of nervousness, but anticipation. The game had begun.

"Lord Farringer, may I introduce Mrs. Clara Woolrich, the widow I told you about," Lady Darlington said. "She was quite eager to meet you."

Quick and to the point, but then we didn't have much time. The elopement was set for a few days from now.

Farringer took my hand, his touch light but deliberate, his eyes never leaving mine. "Mrs. Woolrich, a pleasure to meet you."

Schooling my features into an air of awe, I offered him a trembling smile, "It's an honor to make your acquaintance, Lord Farringer."

"The honor, I assure you, is all mine, Mrs. Woolrich," he said, placing an impeccably manicured hand over his heart.

"Oh, there's Lady Patton," Lady Darlington said. "It's been an age since I've seen her. May I leave Mrs. Woolrich in your capable hands, Lord Farringer?"

"Never fear, milady. I will take good care of her."

And with that, Lady Darlington was off.

"I confess, I've not had the pleasure of seeing you at these sorts of gatherings before," he said. "But then Lady Darlington informed me you're new to London's social scene." His voice was smooth, like silk sliding over glass.

"Indeed, I am," I replied, allowing a touch of shyness to

creep into my voice. "I've only just arrived from the country-side. London is . . . quite a change."

"It can be overwhelming, can it not? Especially for a novice." His smile widened, as if he had found a rare jewel amidst the evening's frivolities.

Only a few days away from marrying the princess, and he was exerting his wiles on a new lady.

"So what brings you to London?" He asked.

I lowered my head. "I wish to marry."

"So soon after your husband's death?"

"My husband died two years ago." I allowed my voice to waver. "Tragically so."

"My condolences."

"That's very kind of you." I allowed a moment to grieve for my nonexistent husband. "We were not blessed with children during our brief six-month marriage. And I so wish for children. That's why I've come to London."

"To find a husband who'll give you a child?" He glanced around in a desperate bid to desert me. I had to hook him quickly before he got away.

I sighed. "I've been told it won't be difficult to find one. I have a fortune, you see."

His head jerked back to me. "A fortune, you say?"

"Yes, my father settled a generous dowry on me when I married. My husband—" A tear ran down my cheek "—well, he barely touched it. And now, with interest, I'm told it has grown. I don't even know the amount at the moment, but I've been told it's considerable. More than 100,000 pounds."

"A hundred thousand pounds?" He squeaked out.

"So I've been told."

"Well, that certainly makes for a very attractive incentive." There was something in his eyes, a calculating gleam that confirmed what I already knew: Farringer wasn't just charming; he was avaricious, dangerous even. "For the right gentleman, that is."

"That's what I hope." I once more lowered my head before glancing up at him again. "I hate to ask such a thing. But do you know of any eligible gentlemen who are eager to marry? I would not be a demanding wife. Just the contrary. As long as I have children and a beautiful home, I will be content. He must have a title, though. My heart is set on becoming a lady."

"I might. Do you dance, Mrs. Woolrich?"

"Yes, of course."

"The next one will be a waltz. Would you care to dance with me?"

"It would be a pleasure, Lord Farringer. But I would rather learn more about you. I've heard about your travels from Lady Darlington and found them fascinating. I've never left Yorkshire, you see. Well, until now." Once more, I glanced shyly at my feet.

"Let us promenade then." Farringer offered me his arm. I hesitated only briefly before accepting. While he led me across the room, I listened attentively as he regaled me with tales of his journeys—extravagant stories of adventures in the Orient, lavish hunting parties on estates across Europe, and encounters with dignitaries and royalty. I knew the type: men who wore their experiences like badges of honor, embellishing every detail for maximum effect. Heaven knew I'd met enough of them during my debut season.

As we strolled through the ballroom, I steered the conversation toward his business ventures, hoping to glean some insight into the man behind the polished façade. "You've seen so much of the world, milord," I remarked. "Surely a man of such diverse experiences must have many enterprises to manage."

Farringer tilted his head slightly, his lips curling into a

small smile as if amused by my curiosity. "Ah, yes. One must always keep busy, Mrs. Woolrich. I have investments in various industries—shipping, textiles, the usual fare for a man of my standing."

I nodded, feigning innocent admiration. "How fascinating. And do you find these ventures fulfilling?"

"Fulfilling?" He glanced at me, as though he were considering whether or not to share more. "I suppose one could say that. But fulfillment is a complex thing, don't you agree? One can have all the wealth and success in the world and still feel . . . incomplete."

I arched an eyebrow, sensing an opportunity. "Incomplete, my lord? What could possibly be missing?"

Farringer paused, his eyes locking onto mine with an intensity that sent a chill down my spine. "Ah, but that is a conversation for another time. I wouldn't want to bore you with such musings on a night like this."

I smiled, though inwardly I made a mental note of his response. Incomplete. There was more to Lord Farringer than met the eye. He was a man with secrets, and I intended to uncover every one of them.

As the evening progressed, Farringer continued his attempts to charm me, but I remained vigilant, carefully steering the conversation whenever possible. All the while, my mind worked behind the scenes, analyzing every word, every gesture. What was he hiding? And what role did he play in the larger plot I had been sent to investigate?

"Ahhh, a waltz. A particular favorite of mine. Now that I've satisfied your curiosity, Mrs. Woolrich, would you care to dance?" Farringer asked, extending his hand.

He would surely suspect something if I denied him once more. So hesitating for only a moment, I accepted. "I'd be delighted, my lord."

As he led me to the dance floor, I had to admit he was an

expert dancer. But then, he'd probably had plenty of opportunities to practice. To an outsider, we probably looked every bit the ideal couple, but beneath the surface, the real game was being played. I had one goal—to get close enough to him to learn the truth, but not so close that I lost myself in the bargain.

As the waltz came to an end, Farringer leaned in, his voice low and intimate. "I have a feeling, Mrs. Woolrich, that you and I will become very good friends."

I smiled, though inwardly I steeled myself. "I do hope so, my lord."

The trap had been set. I had taken my first steps into Farringer's world. Now, all I had to do was wait for him to make his next move.

CHAPTER 5

A GAME OF PRETENSES

While I had been extricating answers from Farringer, Robert had been doing his own bit of sleuthing. Once we returned to the Regent Park residence, and I shed my disguise, we met in the library to discuss the evening's findings. I was not surprised to find myself wide awake. Investigations tended to energize me more than anything else.

Being intensely curious about what he'd discovered, I suggested he go first. Something he was more than happy to do. He'd tracked down Felix Larkspur, one of Farringer's closest business associates, who apparently was known at Scotland Yard for his dubious dealings. Robert had slipped into a side room where he overheard a conversation between Larkspur and another man discussing a shipment of goods that sounded far too secretive to be legitimate.

"Did you get the details of the shipment? Where? When?" I asked.

"Yes, to the where. No to the when. But going by their exchange, I expect it to be soon."

"What's being shipped?"

"That remains to be determined. But I suspect by their demeanor, it's illegal."

"Drugs?"

"Or weapons."

"What would they do with them?"

"They could already have a buyer, of course. They're only middlemen. But if the cargo is valuable enough, they could be holding an auction."

"Where they would sell them to the highest bidder."

"Exactly so. While you were changing, I scribbled out a note about what I'd overheard, and then I asked one of the agents assigned to this enquiry to deliver it to Scotland Yard. He left a few minutes before you walked into the library."

"Goodness. You are efficient. I was only gone for twenty minutes."

He tweaked my chin, a loving gesture of his. "It's what I do, Catherine. Investigate and write reports." He sipped from his whiskey glass. "So what did you find out?"

I shared with him what I'd discovered about Farringer. None of it had been particularly illuminating. But I'd managed to establish a rapport with him. "The mention of the 100,000 pounds certainly caught his attention. But will that be enough to tempt him away from the princess?"

"I believe so. He's fully cognizant of the letter the princess received from her father, and the threat the king made about withholding the dowry. Her fortune does not mean a thing if he can't get his hands on it. Mrs. Woolrich's fortune would be much more attractive to him. It certainly would be enough to pay all his debts."

"But surely he wouldn't rely on only my words? He would need to verify what I've told him."

"The government has taken care of that. They've deposited your 'fortune' in an interest-bearing account at a prestigious bank. If someone were to check, he would find it's all there. And if he were to enquire about your deceased husband, Farringer would discover he did indeed exist and died tragically when he fell off his horse."

"The government can do all that?"

"That and much more."

"So what's next?" I asked.

"Tomorrow you have another ball to attend at which Farringer will be present."

"But what about the princess? He can't exactly pay court to me if she's there."

He swirled what was left of the whisky while glancing away. "Oh, don't worry. She won't be."

I gazed at him with suspicion. "How do you know that? She's not being made ill, is she?"

"Not ill, exactly. A temporary stomach distress. It will last only long enough for you to hook Farringer. Maybe another day or two."

"That's awful."

"I've been assured she'll recover with no ill effects."

"I certainly hope so."

The following evening, Robert and I attended yet another ball. No sooner had we made it past the receiving line than Farringer made a beeline for me. Robert, in his role as the disapproving uncle, frowned at him. But I was quick to reassure him that Lord Farringer was a proper gentleman and introduced him to Robert. Once that charade was performed, Farringer whisked me away to the dance floor.

"Your uncle, is it?" Farringer asked while gracefully

whirling us around the space. I had to admit he was a flawless dancer.

"Yes."

A wrinkle formed across his brow. "He's quite protective of you."

"He believes gentlemen are only interested in my fortune, not myself." I gazed at him with nauseating ardor. "But that's not you, milord. You truly see me for who I am."

"How could I fail to do so, Mrs. Woolrich, when you shine so brightly?" His praise was that of a man who found a woman attractive. But I knew better.

Stiffening up, I said, "That's pouring the butter sauce all over me, Lord Farringer. It will not do. I know I'm not beautiful."

He realized he'd made a mistake, but in the next instant he recovered. "Other women flaunt themselves with flashy gowns and jewelry and excessive maquillage. You do not. You are more like an uncut diamond. It takes a true connoisseur to see the flawless gem hidden deep within."

Goodness. He could dissemble with such charm and lack of guile that one would never suspect he was a liar. Still, I had a part to play. "Why, thank you, Lord Farringer. That's quite the nicest thing any gentleman has said to me."

He squeezed my hand. "I meant it, dear lady."

We ended the evening with him asking if he could call on me the next day. I provided him with the permission he sought and said I would be at home at two.

The following afternoon, he arrived all smiles, carrying a huge bouquet of lilies. Not a surprise on his choice of blooms. I'd expressed my preference for them the night before. I'd requested that tea be served soon after his arrival. In no time at all, a spread of pastries, tea, and coffee lay before us.

"Will your uncle be joining us?" Farringer asked.

"He had an appointment that required his presence. I hope you don't mind I'm unchaperoned."

"Not at all." He hid a smile behind his teacup.

In reality, Robert had gone off to Scotland Yard to expand on the note he'd submitted the night before. Rickard would be there as well, as he wished to question Robert.

In the meantime, Farringer's afternoon call had begun well, but it would not last. I needed to express my displeasure with him.

"It has come to my attention, Lord Farringer, that you have been courting the Princess of Zenovia." I couldn't very well ignore it. Last night during a visit to the restroom, I'd heard several ladies whispering about it. As I walked by them on the way to the private stalls, they'd sent me pitying glances.

Farringer must have been expecting my pronouncement because he had a ready answer. "Not courting, dear lady, befriending her. May I explain?"

I nodded. "Of course."

"The estate where she was staying in the country was located next to mine. One day I met her while horseback riding. I quickly realized she sorely needed a friend. Up to that moment, she only had servants and an older companion assigned to her by her parents. She didn't have the slightest idea how to get on in society, so she asked for my advice. I visited her several times to explain the intricacies of the season. She was extremely grateful."

"Is that all it is? Friendship?"

"On my part. I'm afraid, however, she has come to think of me as something more than that." He shook his head. "My fault, I suppose. I should have realized she mistook my friendship for ardor." He gazed off into the distance and sighed dramatically. "She's been ill the last two days. Although I'm not happy she is not feeling well, I'm glad for the distance. Maybe she'll come to realize I'm not what she wishes me to be."

The cheek of the man! I knew for a fact, he'd obtained a license so he could marry the princess, and that arrangements had been made at a small church just outside London. But of course, as Mrs. Woolrich, I wouldn't know all that.

I offered him a satisfied smile. "Thank you for explaining it to me. Young girls do like to fall in love. She misunderstood your kindness for something more serious."

He bit back a smile. He honestly thought I'd fallen for his explanation. "You're the only lady who holds my attention." He captured my hand and kissed it.

Somehow, I managed a blush. Not because I was pleased, but because I was angry.

His grin told me he was pleased by my reaction. "I'm holding a small dinner party this evening. Only a few friends. May I prevail upon you to attend?"

"I'd love to, but I can't go on my own. My uncle will need to escort me. I hope you understand."

"By all means, the invitation includes him as well."

"In that case, I gladly accept."

After he'd provided me with his address and the time, he came to his feet, bowed over my hand, and made his way out the door.

CHAPTER 6

AN UNEXPECTED THREAT

*H*alf an hour later, Robert returned from Scotland Yard.

"Farringer invited us to supper at his house."

"When?"

"Tonight, at eight. I accepted for both of us."

He scowled.

"You're not jealous, are you?"

"Of course not." All evidence to the contrary. He was acting exactly as a jealous man would.

"Granted he's quite charming and strikingly handsome," I said.

He raised a brow.

I laughed as I wrapped my arms around him. "I'm teasing. You are the only man for me." And then I proceeded to show him how much he meant to me.

A knock on the door sadly interrupted us. The agent

who'd been masquerading as our butler stepped into the room.

"Mrs. Woolrich, Mister Vale, you have visitors."

We both turned to face the lady and gentleman walking in the door. Lord Marlowe and Lady Emma.

"What on earth?" I exclaimed.

Lady Emma approached and kissed my cheek. "I tried to talk Marlowe out of it, but he would not be dissuaded." She took a long, hard look at me. "You look perfectly hideous."

"Thank you." Not only did the blonde wig itch to no end, but my eyebrows were so thick I refused to look at myself in the mirror. And then there was the matter of the extra padding, which made me look two stones heavier.

"Marlowe," Robert said. "What are you doing here?"

"I saw you last night at the ball. Recognized both of you, of course. No one has your walk, Kitty, or your stance, Sinclair."

"Anyone else recognized us?"

"Not as far as I know. But if I were you, I wouldn't make too many public appearances. Sooner or later, someone is bound to recognize you."

Something that would be very hard to do as the romance between Lord Farringer and Mrs. Woolrich had to be conducted in public. The princess could not be convinced to cry off otherwise.

"How did you track us down to this address?" Robert asked.

"I followed you when you left the ball."

Robert frowned. "I'll need to talk to our chauffeur. He should have spotted you."

"So what exactly is going on?" Marlowe asked.

"We can't share that with you," I said.

Marlowe accommodated himself on the settee next to Lady Emma and availed himself of a pastry. "Shall I guess?"

"Stop teasing, Marlowe," Lady Emma admonished before glancing at me. "He knows."

Marlowe was extremely bright. Still, he should not have so much of an inkling about our undercover operation. "How on earth would he know?"

Marlowe polished off the treat and cleaned his hands with one of the napkins. "All society can talk about is the Princess of Zenovia. For the last couple of weeks, she's been seen firmly clinging to Farringer's arm. It is rumored that they're planning to marry. When I saw you being nauseatingly enamored with Farringer, it didn't take me but a moment to figure out what was happening."

I crossed my arms in front of me. "And that is?"

"The princess is expected to marry the man her father, the king, chose for her. Given Farringer's reputation, the king is bound to disapprove of Farringer becoming her husband. Since Zenovia is strategically located, we Brits need to maintain an amicable relationship with the royal family. That is bound to suffer if Farringer does, in fact, marry the princess. So our government is eager to throw a spanner in the works. You, Kitty, in your guise as" —he gestured toward me— "whatever that is supposed to be, are to lure Farringer away from the princess. Since you're not particularly attractive in that guise, I imagine you're quite wealthy."

"Amazing, isn't it?" Lady Emma said. "Marlowe can be quite brilliant when he wishes to be."

Dropping his jesting demeanor, Marlowe gazed adoringly at Lady Emma. "Thank you."

"Of course, that rarely happens."

Marlowe shook his head but kept his smile.

I tossed a worried glance at Robert. "They're verifying what I overheard last night. So much for keeping the elopement a secret."

"Servants talk, Kitty," Lady Emma said.

"Not the Worthington House ones."

"They're quite loyal to your family, a consequence of being well-paid and well-treated. Not every employer is as generous as your father or as kind as your mother."

"So what do we do?" I asked Robert. "Not only are we likely to be recognized in public, but news about the impending elopement is apparently out in the open."

"This operation will need to be over and done with as quickly as possible." He turned to Marlowe and Lady Emma. "Thank you for letting us know. But you need to leave now. Don't let anybody see you on the way out."

"Bye, darling," Lady Emma kissed my cheek. "If you need anything?"

"I'll telephone. It was good to see you. More than you'll know." I had missed our daily meetings with coffee, tea, and biscuits.

Marlowe simply nodded toward Robert before escorting Lady Emma out of the room.

"So how do we proceed?" I asked Robert once they'd gone.

CHAPTER 7

A SHIFT IN TACTICS

*T*hat evening, the princess still must have been under the weather, for she was not present at Farringer's home. No mention was made of her when he greeted me in his drawing room, nor did I ask. I was more concerned over whether either Robert or I would be recognized. As it turned out, I had nothing to fear. None of the guests were familiar to me.

The first couple Farringer introduced us to were Lord and Lady Brightmore. While the husband appeared to be in his late forties, his wife was much younger, in her late twenties would be my guess. Her dismissive glance revealed she thought little of me. We were next introduced to Felix Larkspur who was there with a Mrs. Polin on his arm. Her attire was not exactly *comme il faut*. Quite the contrary. Her décolletage was quite low cut, revealing much more of her abundant charms than was proper. And her *maquillage* appeared to have been spackled on rather than carefully applied. After an excruciating fifteen minutes during which cocktails were served, supper was announced.

The numbers were odd—four gentlemen to three ladies. A circumstance mother would never have allowed. But then Farringer did not seem to be overly concerned with etiquette as he sat me next to him with Robert to my right. Another *faux pas*. Since Lady Brightmore held a title, she should have occupied that place of honor. He had the awful Mrs. Polin seated at the other end of the table with Larkspur by her side and Lady Brightmore and Lord Brightmore next to him.

Somehow, conversation flowed smoothly as the meal progressed, although much of it was not to my liking. Lady Brightmore and Mrs. Polin engaged in town gossip, something I abhorred. Not that I would have had time to engage as Lord Farringer was claiming all my time. Much in the manner of earlier that afternoon, he praised my manners, my dress, and my looks, while leaning close to me. I sensed more than saw Robert's stiffened posture. But he said nothing about Farringer's words. Once the meal ended, Mrs. Larkspur suggested the ladies retire to the drawing room, leaving the men to their port and cigars.

This afternoon, Robert and I had discussed the strategy we would employ. We'd determined this would be the best time for me to do a spot of investigation. I remained in the drawing room for only a few minutes. And then, claiming I needed to visit the restroom, I excused myself.

A hall clock struck eleven as I scurried through the corridors of Farringer House. As agents had reconnoitered the layout of the mansion, I knew exactly where I was headed— the library. Apparently, that was where Farringer kept his business records. Thankfully, I encountered no one on the way there. With barely a click of the door, I made my way into the room.

For a few moments, I stood by the entrance, getting the

lay of the land. A fireplace had been lit, providing enough illumination so I could see into the handsomely appointed room. Books lined the walls on both sides and the back. In the center of it all, an impressive desk presided over the space. If anything were to be found, it would be there. I just hoped the drawers would not be locked.

Taking a deep breath, I tried my hand at the top one on the right. When it opened easily, I breathed a sigh of relief. My hands trembled slightly as I rifled through the drawer. It wasn't the first time I'd searched the home of a suspect. My first investigation into the death of a woman who'd been murdered on the Golden Arrow came to mind. But tonight, the stakes were much higher. The future of a young woman, never mind England, depended on what I could find. The grandfather clock with its constant ticking urged me to hurry. It would be a disaster if I were caught. On the verge of giving up, I came across something hidden in a drawer beneath a pile of correspondence.

A document. An innocuous piece of parchment at first glance, its contents marked with the details of a shipment. But it wasn't just any shipment. As my eyes roved over the paper, a chill ran down my spine. The shipment was listed under an alias—a name that I'd heard before during a previous investigation. It was linked to international arms dealers, a network that trafficked weapons to the highest bidder, regardless of the devastation it caused. And Farringer, it seemed, was not only complicit in these dealings —he was directly involved.

My breath hitched as the gravity of the situation hit me. This wasn't just about stopping a wedding to a foreign princess. It wasn't just about Farringer's ambition or his reputation as a cad. This was something far more sinister. I carefully folded the document and dropped it into the pocket that had been cleverly sewn into my gown.

Slipping out of the library as quietly as I'd entered, I made my way back to the drawing room. I plastered on a smile as I greeted Mrs. Polin and Lady Brightmore. They hardly noticed, so deep into their gossip were they. As they continued their character assassinations of several high-ranking members of society, my mind wandered away from their chatter and malicious laughter and waited anxiously for the gentlemen, most specifically Robert, to join us.

CHAPTER 8

ROMANCE AND DECEPTION

*F*ive minutes after the gentlemen entered the drawing room, I made an excuse to leave.

Farringer showed visible disappointment. "How very dreadful, Mrs. Woolrich. I was hoping to show you more of my house."

The two ladies tittered with laughter as they sent malicious glances in my direction.

Wincing as if with pain, I brushed a hand across my brow. "Another time, my lord. Once I've recovered."

"Yes, of course." Going by his demeanor, he was not pleased.

No doubt he'd been planning to compromise me. Little did he know Kitty Worthington would not have put up with that nonsense. I would have kneed him right in the baubles and hit him over the head. The jig would have been up, of course, but then there was only so much I was willing to do for King and Country.

But for now, I had to continue the charade. I allowed Farringer to escort me to the Farringer House entrance. After Robert's and my outer garments were fetched, he wished me a speedy recovery.

"Thank you. My maid has an excellent nostrum for when I suffer from one of my headaches. That and sleep usually works."

"I will not rest until I see you fully recuperated. May I visit tomorrow to ensure that in fact is so?"

"Yes, of course, my lord."

"Until then." He bowed over my hand and then Robert and I made our way out the door.

Once we were in the government car that had been assigned to us, Robert asked, "You found something?"

I nodded. "Let's wait until we're private," I whispered.

Once we arrived at the Regent's Park residence, we proceeded to the library. Entirely different from the one in Farringer House, the coziness of the room helped me breathe easily once more.

"Catherine," Robert said softly, his voice low. "What did you find?"

I didn't answer right away, instead reaching into my pocket and retrieving the document I had taken from Farringer's library. "I found this tonight. Farringer isn't just involved in shady business dealings, Robert. He's trafficking arms."

Robert's brow furrowed as he unfolded the paper and scanned its contents. His face hardened as the full weight of the revelation sank in. "This changes everything," he murmured. "If the princess moves forward with this marriage, and her father capitulates, Farringer would have access to her family's influence—military, political, economic. He could use it all to funnel weapons and resources into the wrong hands."

I nodded, my voice grim. "Exactly. And that would give him immense power. It's no longer just about stopping a wedding—it's about preventing a larger conspiracy that could destabilize Europe. If these arms fall into the wrong hands, we could be looking at the threat of war."

The realization hung between us, heavy and foreboding. What had started as a mission to protect a princess from an unscrupulous suitor had now escalated into something far more dangerous. We were no longer dealing with just Lord Farringer's personal ambitions; we were standing on the brink of something that could affect the entire continent.

Robert paced for a moment, the light from the lamp casting sharp shadows across his face. He was usually calm, unflappable, but this discovery had shaken him. "We have to find out how deep this goes," he said finally. "If Farringer is working with international arms dealers, there's likely a network involved. We'll need to trace his contacts—find out who else is involved."

I nodded, already thinking of our next steps. "Farringer's guard is starting to come down around me. He's suspicious of others, but with me . . . he's different. I can use that. I can get closer to him, find out more about his dealings."

"I don't like it," Robert said, his voice tight with worry. "The closer you get, the more dangerous it becomes. If Farringer finds out who you really are . . ."

I met his gaze. "We've come this far, Robert. We can't turn back now. I'll be careful, but we have to stop him. Not just for the princess, but for the sake of everything he's likely planning."

There was a long silence as we stood together in the library, the weight of our mission pressing down on both of us. Robert stepped closer, his hand brushing lightly against mine. "I trust you," he said softly, his voice filled with both conviction and concern. "But promise me you'll take every precaution. I can't . . ."

He trailed off, his words hanging in the air. I understood what he meant, even if he couldn't say it. He couldn't lose me. The mission might come first, but our hearts were still entwined, and the danger we faced felt all the more real because of it.

"I promise," I said, my voice equally soft but firm. "But we're in this together. We'll find a way to stop him."

Robert nodded, his hand lingering in mine for a moment longer before he pulled away. "I've been tracking Farringer's associates," he said, shifting back into professional mode. "Felix Larkspur has been involved in a number of questionable business deals. I think he's the key to understanding Farringer's network."

My mind raced as I pieced it all together. "If we can get close to Larkspur, we might be able to uncover more about the arms dealings. Perhaps there's a meeting or transaction we can intercept."

Robert agreed, his expression grim. "I'll continue following Larkspur. See where he leads. But you . . . you'll need to keep Farringer close. Play the role, but don't let him suspect anything."

I knew what he was asking of me, and I knew the risks involved. I had to become someone Farringer trusted, someone he wouldn't question. The thought of drawing even closer to Farringer made my skin crawl, but I knew it was necessary. I had no choice now but to play the game and play it well. That meant pushing my own feelings aside, as well as pushing Robert aside for the time being. The pretense of Mrs. Woolrich had to become more real than ever before.

"I'll get closer to him," I said, my voice steady despite the turmoil within. "But if we're going to take him down, we need to act fast. That new shipment he's anticipating will arrive soon."

Robert nodded. "We have to stop him before that happens. We can't afford to fail."

The weight of our task pressed down on both of us, but there was no turning back now. We were at the point of no return. The stakes had risen, and the danger was real. I had always known the mission was risky, but now the risk felt more personal, more immediate.

I was no longer just playing a part in a high-society drama. I was at the center of a conspiracy that could change the course of nations. And now, more than ever, I had to succeed. Not just for the princess, not just for the mission— but for the man I loved and the world we both sought to protect.

CHAPTER 9

THE PRINCESS'S SECRET

To my great surprise, Lord Farringer did not visit the next afternoon. Instead, he sent a note claiming an important matter had surfaced that he needed to attend to. But he hoped to see me at the Cartsworth ball that evening. He would. Thanks to Mrs. Darlington's efforts, both Robert and I had received an invitation.

That evening the grand halls of the Cartsworth mansion sparkled under the glow of chandeliers, their gilded edges glinting in the soft light. As we arrived, I felt a growing sense of unease. Soon, I found out my instincts were correct. As we descended the steps to the ballroom below, I caught sight of Lord Farringer with a tall, statuesque young lady hanging on to his arm. Clearly, Princess Elena of Zenovia. She was exquisitely dressed in a periwinkle blue silk evening gown. A diamond necklace, no doubt worth a king's ransom, adorned her swan-like neck. The finery did not stop there. A matching diamond bracelet circled her wrist. This was the woman I had been tasked with saving from an ill-advised marriage to the notorious and unscrupulous Lord Farringer. I would do my utmost to succeed.

As soon as we reached the bottom of the staircase, we were approached by Lady Darlington. After kissing me on the cheek, she said, "The princess has recuperated and is in attendance."

"I noticed."

"Walk with me," she said. "I have something important to tell you."

"Of course."

After we reached a secluded spot that was free of guests, she said, "We received intelligence that Lord Farringer visited her this afternoon. Unfortunately, the meeting was held behind closed doors so we were not able to hear what was said. But after the meeting ended, the princess was seen wearing a quite valuable ring. She's wearing it tonight. We've been able to determine it's Farringer's mother's ring."

"So they're formally engaged."

"It appears so."

"That's a disaster."

"Yes. We'll need to figure something out."

"She has to visit the restroom at some time. When she does, I'll follow her. We don't have time to waste. We must alert her to what a disaster her marriage to Farringer would be."

An hour later, my opportunity came up. As the princess wound her way around the ballroom toward a hallway I knew led to the ladies' restroom, I followed her.

The bathroom had been designed during the Victorian era. Composed of two rooms, the sitting room contained couches and chairs where women could rest or chat. You had to traverse that room to reach the one where the private stalls and sinks were located. The sitting room was blessedly empty. So I settled into one of the couches and waited until the princess had taken care of her bodily needs.

Once she emerged from the inner room, I came to my feet and curtsied. "Your Royal Highness."

She arched a brow. "Mrs. Woolrich."

To say I was surprised was an understatement. "You know my name?"

"I've been kept informed."

"I need to talk to you about Lord Farringer."

"I have received plenty of warnings about his supposedly unsavory character. There's nothing you can say that I don't already know." Glancing down at her hands, she twisted the quite stunning diamond and sapphire ring on her finger before fixing a quite steady gaze on me. "There's a reason why I must marry him."

Reason? That hinted at something more than love.

A lady entered the room, putting a stop to our conversation. By necessity, we waited until she walked into the area where the private stalls were located to proceed. Even so, the princess took precautions to ensure her words would not be overheard. Wearing a conspiratorial air as if we had known each other for years rather than moments, she leaned into me.

"Mrs. Woolrich," the princess began, her voice soft but clear, "I am not so naïve as to believe that love is all that matters in a marriage. I have seen my family navigate the treacherous waters of European politics my entire life. My parents' marriage was one of necessity, not affection, and yet they rule a kingdom with strength and wisdom."

I nodded, not entirely surprised by this sentiment, but it was the princess's next words that sent me into an inward spiral of doubt.

"I know what people say about Lord Farringer," the princess continued, her gaze never wavering from mine. "I know his reputation. But there are things at play here that are larger than one man's character. Sometimes we must sacrifice our personal desires for the sake of duty."

Duty. I knew the weight that word carried. But what duty could possibly compel Princess Elena to align herself with a man like Farringer? My instincts told me that something deeper was at work here, something I had not yet uncovered. And that suspicion gnawed at me.

"Duty?" I echoed, playing the part of a curious but uninvolved party. "What duty could be so important that you would overlook Mr. Farringer's . . . faults?"

The princess's expression shifted. A guarded look crossed her face for a brief moment before she answered. "That, Mrs. Woolrich, is something I cannot share in full. But let us just say that Zenovia's future depends on this union."

It was a cryptic answer, but it told me enough. Princess Elena knew more about the situation than anyone had given her credit for. She was not the hapless royal being led astray by a charming scoundrel as we'd all thought. She was a woman caught in a political web, one that I had only begun to glimpse.

I left the sitting room with a renewed sense of purpose . . . and a new challenge. If Princess Elena truly believed that her engagement to Farringer was a matter of duty, how could she be persuaded to break it off? And more importantly, how could I achieve this while maintaining my undercover identity as the unassuming Mrs. Woolrich?

As I returned to the ballroom, my mind raced through possible strategies. I had a delicate balance to maintain. On the one hand, I had to maintain an amicable demeanor with the princess, cultivating trust and drawing out more information. On the other, I had to somehow dismantle the engagement from the shadows without revealing my true motives or risking my cover.

As I reached the ballroom, the gentle hum of conversation and the soft strains of a string quartet filled the air. I moved with ease through the sea of elegantly dressed guests, offering smiles and pleasantries along the way. My eyes, however, were scanning the room for Robert. We'd agreed he would be keeping an eye on Farringer and Larkspur, Farringer's associate.

I finally located him near the edge of the ballroom, engaged in what appeared to be a mundane conversation with a gentleman I did not recognize. When he caught sight of me, his gaze sharpened, and he excused himself from the conversation with a polite bow.

"Catherine," Robert said as he reached me, his tone low but urgent. "I've uncovered something you'll want to hear. Farringer's ties to the black market are worse than we thought. Let us seek a quiet place where we can speak in private."

"Of course. I have news of my own I wish to share."

Skirting the ballroom, we located a corridor that ran parallel to that space. It was not only quieter but devoid of guests. There was bound to be a room where we could hold our discussion. Male voices emanated from the first two doors, but the third one was silent. Taking the lead, Robert turned the knob to find a room blessedly empty. We snuck in and locked the door.

Robert wasted no time in revealing what he'd learned. "As you know, Farringer's been smuggling weapons into the country."

"We knew that from the invoice we found."

"But what we didn't know was what he planned to do with them. I thought he'd sell them to the highest bidder in England, but his plans are more evil than that."

"What do you mean?"

"The weapons will not remain in England. We're only a

temporary stop. As soon as they are received, they will be placed on other ships and transported to ports of entry all over Europe where they will be distributed to dissident groups itching to set off another conflict on the continent."

My heart quickened. This was the leverage we needed. If Farringer was involved in something criminal, surely that would be enough to convince Princess Elena to break the engagement. But then I remembered the princess's words— *Zenovia's future depends on this union.* What if the princess already knew about Farringer's dealings — and still believed the marriage was necessary?

I sighed, my brow furrowing. "Robert, there's more to this than just Farringer's character or his criminal activities. Princess Elena knows who he is, and she's still determined to marry him. She believes it's her duty — something about securing Zenovia's future."

Robert's eyes narrowed in thought. "Duty? That sounds like political maneuvering. Do you think her family is pressuring her?"

"Perhaps," I replied, my voice quiet but steady. "Or maybe there's something else. The princess didn't elaborate, but whatever it is, she's convinced that this marriage is necessary. We need to find out why."

Robert nodded, his expression grave. "If it's a political arrangement, there's likely something bigger at play. Farringer may be using the engagement to gain influence or power. If we can expose his criminal activities, we might be able to stop the marriage before it's too late."

My mind was already whirling with possibilities. If Farringer was seeking power through his connection to the Zenovian royal family, there had to be a way to bring his true intentions to light. But how could we do so without endangering our mission or revealing our roles as government agents?

"We'll need proof," I said, my voice firm. "Something concrete that links Farringer to his illicit activities. If we can obtain that, she'd be free to end the engagement."

Robert nodded. "Agreed. I'll see what I can dig up on Farringer's business associates. In the meantime, keep working on the princess. If you can get her to confide in you further, we may find out what's really driving her to stay in this engagement."

I took a deep breath, steeling myself for the challenge ahead. Convincing the princess to walk away from a marriage she believed was her duty would not be easy, especially when I couldn't reveal my true identity. But I had no choice. The fate of a princess — and perhaps even a kingdom — rested in my hands.

The true crisis, it seemed, had only just begun.

CHAPTER 10

THE TRUTH REVEALED

*T*he early morning mist clung to the view from my window, casting a pale veil over Regent's Park. I stood looking out across the gardens, lost in thought.

The previous night had been a whirlwind of social pleasantries, veiled glances, and secretive exchanges. Upon our return to the residence, Robert had found a note from Rickard waiting for him. After a quick read, he simply said, "I have to go," with no further explanation other than, "Don't wait for me."

Easier said than done. I'd come up to my room and, with the help of my maid, changed out of my hideous disguise. I'd left word I was to be awakened once Robert returned. I hadn't been, which meant he'd either countermanded my order or had never made it home. My first thought upon awakening had been to find out if he had indeed returned. I was assured he had—at five this morning.

Given that response, I couldn't wake him. He needed his

rest. So I had to wait for hours for him to rise. Unfortunately, patience was not one of my virtues. Finally, at eleven I was summoned to the library where he stood, handsome as ever. The mantle of deep weariness he wore over his bones wordlessly informed me the news would not be good.

But my first concern was his well-being. "How are you?"

He shrugged. "I'll live."

"Well, that certainly is an ominous beginning. What happened last night?"

"I ordered coffee. Let's wait until it's served for us to talk."

"By all means." I much preferred coffee over tea, a habit I'd adopted during my days at the Swiss finishing school.

Not five minutes later, the coffee service arrived. After I poured cups for both of us, he spoke, "Several months ago, British intelligence discovered a smuggling ring, spanning from England to continental Europe. The weapons come into England and then are distributed to several ports throughout the continent."

"For what purpose?" I asked.

"A substantial number of soldiers who served during the Great War were not pleased with the Treaty of Versailles. They believe Germany should have been annihilated rather than being given a light slap on the wrist. They have organized militias in many European countries. They plan to induce chaos in every capital, from Madrid to Rome to Paris and so on. Their aim is to topple governments and seize power. British and European intelligence knew about it. But the dissidents were not taken seriously. You see, they didn't have the weapons to achieve their goals."

"But now they would."

"Yes. British Intelligence knew there was a shadowy figure operating in the background. But they did not know who the mastermind was. The letter you found in Farringer's study provided the proof they needed to finally identify him."

A chill ran up my spine. "But why would he do this?"

"He plans to declare himself emperor of all Europe."

"That could never happen."

"Probably not all of Europe. But he'd probably succeed in some of the smaller countries."

"Such as Zenovia."

"More than likely."

"Well, that explains why the princess is willing to marry him. She thinks by doing so, she will save her country."

"An erroneous assumption. Once his militias vanquish the Zenovian troops, his first order of business will be to murder the King and Queen."

"The same thing that happened in Russia. The Bolsheviks assassinated Tsar Nicholas II and his entire family." My heart raced with the enormity of what he'd discovered. "So what is the government going to do about it?"

"We know when the next shipment will arrive and where. Farringer meets every one. This is the largest one of all. So he will more than likely be present."

"When will this happen?"

"Tomorrow night. British forces will be there to greet him. They will seize the ship and the cargo. And, of course, arrest him."

"Such shipments must have happened before."

"They have."

"Why weren't they intercepted by Customs?"

"He paid off the Customs officials. They will be arrested as well, but we have to allow this last shipment to take place."

"What I don't understand is the princess's role in this."

"His engagement to her is part of his cover. No one would suspect him of being a smuggler when he was busy romancing the princess. Everyone thought he was only a cad." Robert crossed his arms, his expression grim. "There's more. Farringer knows about us."

I froze, my eyes locking onto Robert's. "What do you mean?"

"He knows who you are, who we both are." Robert's voice was tight. "I don't know how, but he's known for a while. He's been playing us."

A chill crept down my spine. Farringer had known all along? I thought of every conversation I'd had with him, every carefully orchestrated smile and nod. I thought I'd been the one watching him, but all along, Farringer had been watching me too.

"Our part in this charade is done," Robert said. "British intelligence will take over from here. You can return home."

"No, I'm afraid I can't."

His brow wrinkled.

"I received a note from the princess. The wedding is to take place tomorrow afternoon. We have to stop it before it takes place."

CHAPTER 11

A RACE AGAINST TIME

Once more disguised as Mrs. Woolrich, I stepped out of the black government automobile. My gloved fingers tightened on the handle of my handbag, not out of nervousness but with the thrill of the challenge ahead. I pulled up the collar of my fur-trimmed coat up against the brisk March wind, glancing once more at the small gold watch pinned to my bodice.

Time was of the essence. Every minute spent lingering outside the townhouse where the princess was residing meant a greater chance of discovery. But I had no time for second thoughts. The future of the Princess of Zenovia, and perhaps the political fate of Britain, hinged on this operation.

I made my way briskly to the front entrance of the princess's temporary residence, where two guards in dark coats stood.

As I approached, one of the guards, a tall man with a

slightly crooked nose, blocked my path. "What's your business, ma'am?" he asked, eyeing me with a mixture of suspicion and politeness.

I gave him a warm smile, the kind that made me appear harmless and utterly ordinary. "Mrs. Woolrich," I said with a slight nod, giving just enough of an imperious tone to suggest I was not used to being questioned. "I have an appointment with Her Highness, Princess Elena of Zenovia. We're to do a little shopping for some, shall we say, delicate necessities ahead of her wedding day."

The guard hesitated for only a moment before stepping aside. My practiced demeanor and impeccable attire left little room for doubt. Besides, who would dare suspect an upper-class woman of kidnapping a princess?

Inside, the drawing room was grand but austere, far too impersonal to be a permanent residence. But then, it had only been rented for the season. The butler led me to where the princess awaited. With her dark, lustrous hair and regal bearing, Princess Elena could not be mistaken for anything less. Yet, there was something vulnerable about her, a look in her eyes that spoke of uncertainty and unease.

"Ah, Mrs. Woolrich, how good of you to come," the princess said with a slight bow of her head.

I smiled, stepping closer. "It is an honor, Your Highness. I'm sure you must be terribly busy with wedding preparations, but I thought a short excursion might lighten your spirits."

The princess blinked, curiosity evident. "What sort of excursion?"

I leaned in slightly, lowering my voice conspiratorially. "Well, it occurred to me that a bride should have the finest of . . . undergarments for her wedding night. No expense spared, of course. I have just the perfect dressmaker who specializes in such things. A private fitting, completely discreet."

The princess hesitated, her eyes flickering with uncertainty. I seized the moment, my voice becoming softer, warmer. "It's a small indulgence, a gift to yourself before the grand occasion. Just an hour or two, then I shall have you back here, none the wiser."

The princess bit her lip, glancing toward the window where a heavy velvet curtain partially obscured the dreary London streets. I could see her mind working, likely turning over the mounting pressure of her upcoming marriage to Lord Farringer—a man I knew to be utterly vile and not at all what he presented himself to be.

"Very well," Princess Elena said at last. "It might be nice to step out for a little while."

I hid a sigh of relief and motioned to the butler. "We'll be just a short while, no need to accompany us."

Within minutes, we were out the door and into the waiting automobile. The princess chatted nervously about her upcoming nuptials, oblivious to the true nature of the errand we were embarking on. I kept the conversation light, steering the car toward the dressmaker's shop where the next part of the plan was set in motion.

THE SMALL DRESSMAKER'S shop in the heart of Mayfair had been carefully chosen. Known for its exclusive clientele, it was the sort of place where a princess could slip in and out without drawing undue attention. I led the princess inside, where the dressmaker awaited us.

The fitting itself was all a pretense, of course. As the princess stepped behind a folding screen to try on a silk nightgown, I exchanged a subtle glance with the dressmaker. Everything was in place. The plan was for Princess Elena to leave the shop through the back alley, where an intelligence agent was waiting with another car.

I pretended to fuss over lace details and delicate ribbons as I guided the princess toward the back of the shop. "Just a moment, Your Highness, we'll have you fitted for a second gown. This way, please."

With perfect timing, the door to the alleyway opened, and the princess stepped through, unknowing that her path was no longer toward a wedding night but away from it. I followed behind, glancing briefly down the street to ensure we hadn't been followed. The car awaited us, engine idling softly, and the agent at the wheel gave me a curt nod.

"What is this?" The princess asked.

The dressmaker approached with a warm coat which she tossed over the princess. We couldn't very well have Her Highness parading around in nothing but a nightgown.

"A precaution," I said buttoning the coat. "The driver noted a suspicious character while you were trying on the nightgown. We thought it best if we left through the back door. Please climb into the automobile, your Highness, before we are seen."

As we pulled away from the dressmaker's, my heart quickened. The princess was now safely in British Intelligence custody. Soon we would reach Worthington House, where the final stage of the plan would unfold.

My home was quiet when we arrived, save for a few trusted staff members who were in on the scheme. After we made our way through the house's back entrance, I led the princess up the back staircase to a room with no windows. Mother awaited us inside the room, a warm but firm figure ready to greet the displaced royal.

She wasted no time introducing herself. "My dear, I'm

Mrs. Worthington, Kitty's mother. You are safe now," Mother said with a kind smile, taking Princess Elena by the hand.

Princess Elena, still somewhat bewildered by the sudden change of events, looked between the two of us, a look of fear in her eyes. "Kitty? Safe? What . . . what is happening?"

I stepped forward, my expression serious. "Your Highness, my real name is Catherine Worthington, Kitty to friends and family. This is my mother, Mrs. Worthington. You were about to be forced into a marriage that could have destroyed your future. Lord Farringer is not the man he pretends to be. We have removed you from his reach—for your own protection and your family's."

For a moment, the princess looked as if she might protest, but then she sank into the nearest chair, her shoulders slumping as if a great weight had been lifted from them. "I never wanted this marriage," she whispered. "But I had no choice."

"Now you do," I replied gently. "And you have powerful allies on your side."

I spent the next hour explaining exactly what Farringer was and the danger he posed to her family, England, and indeed all of Europe. By the end of my recitation, Princess Elena finally relaxed.

SEVERAL HOURS PASSED, the tension in the house thick as we waited for the inevitable confrontation. Just before dusk, the doorbell rang. It was not unexpected. Farringer would come looking for his bride.

I descended the staircase with deliberate poise, my expression schooled into polite neutrality. Farringer stood in the middle of the drawing room, his face twisted in thinly veiled fury. Mother was seated on her favorite sofa, calmly taking in the scene.

"Kitty, dear. Lord Farringer seems to think we're holding his fiancée, the Princess of Zenovia, prisoner."

"Where is she?" he demanded, not bothering with pleasantries.

I tilted my head, affecting an air of innocence. "I'm afraid I don't know what you're talking about, my lord. I have never met the princess, nor have I met you."

"Don't play games with me, Miss Worthington," Farringer spat. "The princess. She's gone missing, and I know you had something to do with it."

I smiled sweetly, batting my lashes. "Surely you don't think I would be involved in such a scandalous affair."

Farringer's temper flared, and he took a menacing step toward me. "I'll have you arrested for this!"

I placed my hands on his shoulders and drove my knee into his groin. Farringer doubled over, gasping in pain, while I stepped back with perfect composure.

Mother rose to her feet and rang for Carlton, our butler. "I think it's time you left our home, Lord Farringer. You've caused quite enough of a scene."

Farringer could only hiss through gritted teeth as Carlton appeared beside him.

"Shall I escort him out, madam?" Carlton asked Mother with a slight bow.

"Please do," she replied.

With great dignity, Carlton took Farringer by the arm and half-carried, half-dragged him out of the drawing room to the Worthington House entrance. A moment later, we heard the heavy front door slammed shut behind him.

Smiling widely, I turned to Mother. "Well, that went rather well, don't you think?"

Mother nodded in approval. "Indeed, my dear. Indeed."

As Mother and I made our way upstairs to where the princess awaited news, I couldn't help but feel a sense of triumph. The princess was safe, Farringer was out of the picture, and the marriage had been thwarted. Now, all that remained was to see how the game would continue to unfold.

CHAPTER 12

A NEW BEGINNING

The clock on the mantel ticked relentlessly, each second stretching into an eternity as I paced the length of my private sitting room. The night before had been a whirlwind—frenzied whispers, covert operations, and a rush of adrenaline that left my mind racing long after the events had played out. Now, the morning was dragging on without a word, and the uncertainty gnawed at me. I needed to know how it all had ended.

The princess was safely tucked away in one of the guest rooms, contentedly occupied with a mountain of books from the Worthington library. Apparently, Princess Elena of Zenovia had a voracious appetite for reading, a trait that had surprised me when she had shyly asked for something to pass the time.

Mother, of course, had been only too pleased to oblige. I'd carefully chosen a selection of books and had them delivered to her room, everything from romance novels to historical accounts. The princess, it seemed, was particularly enamored with poetry, though she had also taken a keen interest in political treatises, a fact that amused me to no end.

At least someone was having a peaceful morning.

My thoughts, however, remained on the secret operation from the night before—the seizure of weapons from a clandestine cache, part of a plot far larger than I had initially realized. Weapons that, had they fallen into the wrong hands, could have sparked a conflict that would ripple across Europe. And Farringer . . . I shuddered at the thought of the man. He had been far more dangerous than I had anticipated, his ambitions stretching beyond mere personal gain. I desperately needed to hear from Robert. Until I did, I would find no rest.

At last, a knock came at the door. As I practically leaped to answer it, my heart skipped a beat.

"Lord Robert has arrived, Miss," my maid, Grace, said. "He offers his compliments and asks that you meet him in the drawing room."

I could have kissed the woman.

After racing down the stairs, I burst into the drawing room to find Robert standing there, his expression as composed as ever but with the familiar spark of humor in his eyes.

"Robert!" I exclaimed, my relief palpable as I rushed toward him. "I've been waiting all morning. Please, tell me everything."

Taking my hands in his, he guided me to a sofa where we both took a seat. "I had to come in person. There's much to discuss, and it's not the sort of thing I'd trust to a message."

"I understand." I squeezed his hand.

"For your ears only," he added quietly, the weight of his words unmistakable.

I sat, my fingers nervously fiddling. "Go on, then," I urged. "Tell me what happened."

Resting his elbows on his knees, Robert leaned forward, his voice low and serious. "The operation was a success. The weapons were seized late last night, just as we planned. Farringer's men never saw it coming. By the time they realized what was happening, it was too late."

I let out a small breath of relief. "And Farringer?"

"Arrested." Robert's mouth curved into a grim smile. "He didn't put up much of a fight once his plans were foiled. I suspect he thought his position would protect him, that someone would intervene on his behalf. But he miscalculated. The entire thing is being kept under wraps, as you might expect. None of this will be made public."

I frowned slightly. "So no trial? No justice?"

"There will be justice," Robert assured me. "But it will be handled quietly. Farringer's arrest is just the beginning. Even as we speak, the leaders of this conspiracy are being rounded up across Europe. The governments have acted swiftly, forming an alliance of sorts to prevent any further plots. They are watching for signs of secret troop gatherings, hidden caches of weapons, anything that might suggest a larger scheme."

I nodded slowly, understanding the gravity of the situation. "A new alliance? But between whom?"

"Several nations," Robert replied. "Britain, France, and a few others. Each country will have someone in place, someone who can keep abreast of any movements or suspicious activities. It's all very secretive, of course, but the aim is to prevent another disaster like this from happening in the future."

My mind raced with the implications of such an alliance. "They asked you to be involved, didn't they?" I could tell by the way he was speaking that something more personal had transpired.

Robert's eyes met mine, and he gave me a small nod. "Yes, they did. They wanted me to head up the British side of things. But I declined."

"You declined?" My surprise was evident. "Why?"

Robert's expression softened. "I've had my fill of the intelligence business, Catherine. I know my way around it, and I'm good at it, but . . . it's not where I want to be. There's too much grey, too many unknowns. At Scotland Yard, at least I know who the villains are. I can do my work, bring criminals to justice, and go home with a clear conscience."

I smiled at him, understanding. "You prefer the straightforward path. I can't say I blame you."

Robert lightly brushed his thumb over my knuckles. "Now that the danger has passed, I thought we might focus on more pleasant things. Like supper."

I chuckled softly. "I think we've earned it, don't you?"

With that, I had to agree.

THAT EVENING, the Worthington House dining room was filled with light and laughter. The tensions of the past days had melted away, and the entire household seemed to breathe easier knowing the princess was safe and the plot had been thwarted.

Princess Elena joined us for supper, her demeanor far more relaxed than when she had first arrived. Freed from the burden of her impending marriage to Farringer, she appeared younger, almost carefree. She had spent much of the day in her room, devouring the books she had requested, but now she was ready to socialize.

"I must say," Princess Elena remarked as she took her seat

at the table, "your library is simply extraordinary. I had no idea you had such a collection."

Kitty smiled warmly. "I'm glad you found it to your liking. You're welcome to borrow as many books as you like for as long as you're here."

The princess beamed. "I've already made a list of the ones I'd like to take with me when I return home. Not yours, of course. Ones I'll purchase."

Just about every member of my family was there. Mother and Father, my brother Ned, Margaret, newly married to Sebastian, the Duke of Wynchcombe. The only one missing was Richard, who was in Egypt. Also present were Marlowe and Lady Emma, Lady Lily and Lady Mellie, as well as her brother, the ever-charming Hollingsworth, who thankfully knew nothing of the covert operation. He would resent the fact that Marlowe had winkled it out while he had no clue.

Supper was a lively affair, filled with easy conversation and delicious food. The room echoed with laughter as Hollingsworth regaled us with stories of his most recent escapades, some of which involved an absurd amount of champagne and questionable company. He was a sailor. Need I say more?

As the evening wore on, I found myself seated beside Robert, the two of us speaking in low tones about our future. The danger had passed, and now we could finally focus on what came next.

"I was thinking," Robert said, a teasing glint in his eye, "that we should throw you a birthday party. Something grand, in honor of everything you've accomplished lately."

I raised an eyebrow. "A birthday party?"

"At Gennaro's," he added, referring to London's swankiest jazz club. "It's been a while since we had a proper celebration, don't you think?"

Kitty's lips curved into a smile. "Gennaro's, hmm? I suppose I could be persuaded." Secretly, I was thrilled.

"Good," Robert said with a wink. "I'll make the arrangements. A night of dancing, music, and laughter is exactly what we need after all this."

As the evening drew to a close and the last of the guests said their goodbyes, Robert and I lingered by the fire, our hands entwined, quietly planning a future filled with love, adventure, and, for once, a little peace.

But as I glanced at the flickering flames, a sense of excitement bubbled within me. Life, as always, had a way of throwing unexpected challenges my way. I couldn't wait to see what the next chapter would bring.

DID you enjoy "The Case of the Unsuitable Suitor"? The Kitty Worthington Cozy Capers is a spinoff of the very popular Kitty Worthington Mysteries. If you haven't yet read that series, you might wish to start with **Murder on the Golden Arrow**, Book 1 in the Kitty Worthington Mysteries, available on Amazon and Kindle Unlimited

What's a bright young woman to do when her brother becomes the main suspect in a murder? Why, solve the case, of course.

England. 1923. After a year away at finishing school, where she learned etiquette, deportment, and the difference between a salad fork and a fish one, Kitty Worthington is eager to return home. But minutes after she and her brother Ned board the Golden Arrow, the unthinkable happens. A woman with a mysterious connection to her brother is poisoned, and the murderer can only be someone aboard the train.

When Scotland Yard hones on Ned as the main suspect, Kitty sets out to investigate. Not an easy thing to do while juggling the demands of her debut season and a mother intent on finding a suitable, aristocratic husband for her.

With the aid of her maid, two noble beaus, and a flatulent basset hound named Sir Winston, Kitty treads a fearless path through the glamorous world of high society and London's dark underbelly to find the murderer. For if she fails, the insufferable Inspector Crawford will most surely hang a noose around her brother's neck.

A frolicking historical cozy mystery filled with dodgy suspects, a dastardly villain, and an intrepid heroine sure to win your heart, Murder on the Golden Arrow is Available on Amazon and Kindle Unlimited

Or maybe you'd like to read Murder in the Mistletoe Shoppe, the next book in the Kitty Worthington Mysteries.

Kitty Worthington's joyous Christmas season spirals into a deadly mystery when a holiday shop owner is murdered, and a dear friend becomes a suspect.

London. 1924. Kitty Worthington, newly married to **Chief Detective Inspector Robert Crawford Sinclair**, is eagerly anticipating spending Christmas with her family at Wynchcombe Castle. But when the health of Robert's brother takes a turn for the worse, their holiday plans change.

Hoping to make their Christmas in London as merry as possible, she visits the city's famous Mistletoe Shoppe to purchase festive decorations. But when she arrives at the emporium, she discovers a chilling scene—the body of the shop owner, with a marionette carved with the name of someone dear to her clutched in his hand.

In no time at all, her treasured acquaintance becomes the main suspect, leaving Kitty with no choice but to investigate. Soon, she discovers the victim was a spy during the Great War. But was he working for the British or the Germans? And how is her friend connected to it all?

With each revelation, Kitty uncovers hidden motives, deceptive alliances, and long-buried betrayals, all set against the backdrop of a snowy London during the holiday season. Can she untangle the truth before her beloved friend pays a horrible price?

Join Kitty Worthington on a journey of suspense and intrigue in this gripping Christmas historical cozy mystery. Murder in the Mistletoe Shoppe, Book 11 in the Kitty Worthington Mysteries, is sure to please fans of Verity Bright and Isabella Bassett.

CAST OF CHARACTERS

Kitty Worthington - Our amateur sleuth

The Ladies of Distinction Detective Agency
Lady Emma Carlyle - Agency Partner
Betsy Robson - Agency Receptionist
Lady Aurelia Holmes - Assistant Lady Detective
Owen Clapham - former Scotland Yard detective inspector who assists with investigations

The Worthington Family
Edward Worthington - Kitty's Father
Mildred Worthington - Kitty's Mother
Carlton - The Worthington House Butler

Other Notable Characters

Detective Inspector Robert Crawford - Kitty's fiancé
Lord Marlowe - An Earl
Phillip Rickard - Under Secretary of Foreign Affairs

Her Royal Highness Princess Elena of Zenovia
Lady Darlington - A Co-conspirator in the scheme
Lord Farringer - Princess Elena's Unsuitable Suitor
Felix Larkspur - an associate of Lord Farringer's

Printed in Great Britain
by Amazon

51420035R00047